Little Ree
Best Friends Forever!

Written by **Ree Drummond**

Illustrated by **Jacqueline Rogers**

HARPER

An Imprint of HarperCollinsPublishers

Little Ree: Best Friends Forever!
Text copyright © 2018 by Ree Drummond
Illustrations copyright © 2018 by Jacqueline Rogers
All rights reserved. Manufactured in China.

ISBN 978-0-06-245319-8 (trade bdg.) — ISBN 978-0-06-282077-8 (special edition)

The artist used pen and ink and watercolors to create the illustrations for this book.
Typography by Rachel Zegar
17 18 19 20 21 SPC 10 9 8 7 6 5 4 3 2 1 ❖ First Edition

When cooking, it is important to keep safety in mind. Children should always ask
permission from an adult before cooking and should be supervised by an adult in the
kitchen at all times. The publisher and author disclaim any liability from any injury that
might result from the use, proper or improper, of the recipe contained in this book.

To Hyacinth, who's always ready for any adventure!
—Ree

For my bestie from first grade, dear Helen
—Jackie

I have a new friend. Her name is Hyacinth. Our grandmas are the best of friends, and now we're the best of friends, too!

Hyacinth is the greatest! She's a country girl
like me, and we like to do exactly the same things.

We like to laugh.

We like to play dress up.

We like to play with
Puggy and Patches,

and we like ridin' the range
and ropin' cattle.
That's what cowgirls do!

If only we knew how to saddle a horse.

And, boy, do we LOVE to bake. The grandmas say what we really love to do is make a mess! We say it just takes a lot of practice to get it right. Right now we are learning to make pie. Our favorite thing!

I'm good at rolling, and Hyacinth likes to make shapes from the dough. We're a great team!

Grandma thinks someday we'll be champion pie makers.
I think we need a little more practice.

Grandma just got back from town! Hyacinth and I always help her carry the groceries. Everybody pitches in on a ranch!

Today Grandma is super excited. There's going to be a pie-baking contest tomorrow! She says Hyacinth and I should enter!

Oh, this will be FUN. We better get cracking!

First we have to decide what pie to make. We know! We'll make
H&R's Country Berry Blast Special! Hyacinth says there are lots
of wild berries to pick on the ranch. This will be perfect!

As berry-picking country girls, we must wear the proper attire.

Boots? Check.
Hats? Check.
Berry basket? Check.
Cute hair? Check!

And . . . a few other things.
Are you ready to go get
berries, Hyacinth?
C'mon, Puggy and
Patches—you can go, too!

Now we just need to find where the berry bushes are. Hyacinth says just look for critters because critters love juicy berries! Good idea!

Ack! There's a critter!

I sure hope he doesn't find our berry bushes.

Look at all those birds!

"Birds love berries," Hyacinth says. "We just have to get across the creek so we can take a look."

Hyacinth tells me crossing the creek is a cinch, but I think it's a muddy mess! She takes my hand and helps me along. "C'mon, Ree," Hyacinth says. "We'll get through this together!"

My boots are going to need a bath.

This is harder than we thought. And there are no berries on these bushes! "Maybe this wasn't such a good idea," I say. "Maybe we should just go home and bake another type of pie."

"No way!" says Hyacinth. "Country girls never give up! And look—Pepper is into something over there."

BERRY BUSHES!!!

And there are so many of them.

"Let's get to picking, Hyacinth," I say. "There's no time to waste!"

"I think we need a little berry snack first," Hyacinth says.

Yum!

Goodness, we have so many berries! We have to get home and start baking—now!

I think we picked too many berries, Hyacinth.

Shoo, Pepper. These berries aren't for you.

Shoo, quail! We need these for our pie!

We'll never get these berries home!
I know—let's tie our bandannas over the top to keep the
critters out. We country girls have to think on our feet!

The grandmas are here. Whew! Can you give a couple
of country girls a lift? We would walk, of course … but
we've got a pie to bake!

Grandmas are the best!

Ready, set,

let's bake pie!

Now THAT is one juicy pie! Uh-oh . . . it doesn't look so good.

I know—we will use some of Hyacinth's shapes.
We will win the prize for originality!

See you at the contest tomorrow, Hyacinth.
Let's wear our matching outfits, OK?

We're here!
We're here!

Let's do this thing, Hyacinth! I think everyone will go
crazy for our H&R's Country Berry Blast Special!

Wow. Look at all the pies. So many flavors and colors.
And some of them are fancy! Our pie isn't fancy.

Oh boy ... the judges are tasting.

And ... judging!

Time for the prizes.
Hold my hand, Hyacinth.
We'll get through this together.

We got 2nd place! HOORAY!

Two is better than one anyway!

Wait, who won 1st?

Hey, look, it's Grandma and Grandma! They made their BFF Banana Cream Bonanza. That's cause they're best friends forever, just like we are.

They won—this time. Next year, watch out—there are new best friends on the block. I mean on the RANCH!

H&R's Country Berry Blast Special!

Serves 8

Pay attention! When you use an oven, especially a very hot one, you need to be extra careful. Always have an adult in the kitchen and never touch the oven or the hot pie plate without oven mitts. Let the adult put the pie in the oven and take it out. Bubbly pie juice is hot and sticky, so don't touch the pie plate or baking sheet after the pie comes out until it cools.

Ingredients

3 cups blueberries (cleaned and dried)

¼ cup sugar, plus extra for sprinkling

2 tablespoons cornstarch

Juice of half a lemon

1 teaspoon lemon zest (it's better if you zest the lemon before you cut it for the juice)

1 teaspoon vanilla extract

Pinch of salt

1 package store-bought piecrust (2 rounds of dough), thawed in the refrigerator

1 large egg

1 tablespoon water

Instructions

1. Have an adult preheat the oven to 425 degrees. Be super careful with a hot oven! Have someone with you in the kitchen all the time.

2. In a bowl, gently stir together blueberries, sugar, cornstarch, lemon juice, lemon zest, vanilla extract, and salt in a bowl. Just let the mixture sit on the side after you combine everything.

3. Unroll the two pieces of dough. Lay one piece into the bottom of a 9- or 10-inch pie pan. Pour in the blueberry mixture. Lay the second piece of dough on top, tucking the top part under the outside edge of the bottom part. Use a fork to press together the edges of the crust against the rim of the pie pan. That's called crimping.

4. Beat the egg and water to make an egg wash. Brush the pie with the egg wash and sprinkle it with a little bit of sugar.

5. Ask an adult to help you cut vents in the top of the pie with a small, sharp knife. Place the pie on a rimmed baking sheet and lightly cover the top with foil and have an adult carefully put the sheet with the pie in the oven. Use mitts—the oven is hot!

6. Bake for 20 minutes, then have an adult remove the foil and bake for another 10–15 minutes, or until the crust is golden and the filling is bubbly. Have an adult carefully remove the hot, bubbly pie from the oven. The pie will be hot, hot, hot, so let it sit and cool for 20 minutes before serving!